VIRAGO
MODERN CLASSICS
644

P. L. Travers was born Helen Lyndon Goff in 1899 in Queensland, Australia. She worked as a dancer and an actress, but writing was her real love and she turned to journalism. Travers set sail for England in 1924 and became an essayist, theatre and film critic, and scholar of folklore and myth. While recuperating from a serious illness Travers wrote *Mary Poppins* – 'to while away the days, but also to put down something that had been in my mind for a long time,' she said. It was first published in 1934 and was an instant success. *Mary Poppins* has gone on to become one of the best-loved classics in children's literature and has enchanted generations. In addition to the *Mary Poppins* books, Travers wrote novels, poetry and non-fiction. She received an OBE in 1977 and died in 1996.

THE FOX AT
THE MANGER

P. L. Travers

THE FOX AT
THE MANGER

P. L. Travers

Engravings by Thomas Bewick

virago

VIRAGO

This edition published in Great Britain in 2015 by Virago Press

3 5 7 9 10 8 6 4 2

First published in Great Britain in 1963 by Collins

Copyright © Trustees of the P. L. Travers Trust, 1963

Engravings by Thomas Bewick courtesy of the
Natural History Society of Northumbria, Great North Museum

The moral right of the author has been asserted.

A CIP catalogue record for this book
is available from the British Library.

ISBN 978-0-34900-571-3

Typeset in Baskerville by M Rules
Printed and bound in Great Britain by
Clays Ltd, St Ives plc

Papers used by Virago are from well-managed forests
and other responsible sources.

MIX
Paper from
responsible sources
FSC® C104740

Virago
An imprint of
Little, Brown Book Group
Carmelite House
50 Victoria Embankment
London EC4Y 0DZ

An Hachette UK Company
www.hachette.co.uk

www.virago.co.uk

To C. to remind him
of his childhood

Author's Note

This story is based on fact and fancy and the characters are fictitious, but only in the sense that people in fairy tales are fictitious. In the land that lies east of the sun and west of the moon they may perhaps be true. For the facts of that world are the legends of ours. In this book I make grateful acknowledgements – first, to Anon., begetter of all legends, for the idea that on Christmas night the animals are given the power of speech; and secondly, to Thomas Bewick, born 1753, dead since 1828, and living ever as the skillful, loving master-engraver of bird and beast.

P. L. T.

THE FOX AT
THE MANGER

CAROL OF THE FRIENDLY BEASTS

Jesus, our brother, strong and good
Was humbly born in stable rude
And the friendly beasts around him stood,
Jesus, our brother, kind and good.

I, said the donkey, shaggy and brown,
Carried his Mother uphill and down
I carried her safe to Bethlehem town,
I, said the donkey, shaggy and brown.

I, said the cow, all white and red,
Gave him my manger for his bed,

I gave him my hay to pillow his head,
I, said the cow, all white and red.

I, said the sheep with curly horn,
Gave him my wool to keep him warm,
He wore my coat on Christmas morn,
I, said the sheep with curly horn.

I, said the dove, in the rafters high,
Cooed him to sleep with lullaby,
We cooed him to sleep, my mate and I,
I, said the dove, in the rafters high.

Thus every beast by some good spell
In the stable dark was glad to tell
Of the gift he gave Immanuel,
Of the gift he gave Immanuel.

From an old Carol

No-ow-ell, No-ow-ell,
No-ow-ell, No-ow-eh-eh-ell
Born is the ki-ing of I-is-ra-el.

sang the choir, like musical news-boys, flinging their glad tidings all round the cathedral and up into the great dark dome.

Silence fell like a thunder-clap, stirred only by a shuffle of black boots under red skirts, and a decorous, almost apologetic, clearing of throats – ahem, ahem, all down the line.

Then the choir-master raised his finger. As though hypnotised, the choir gazed at it, gathering breath for the next effort. The finger wagged – one, two! And the bearers of the tale – so old, so new – were off again in full cry with another version of it.

The candles were steady in their hands, the flames bent sideways with the wind of their singing, and the carol of *The Friendly Beasts* pulsed sweetly through the nave, rising and falling like a lullaby. St Paul's cathedral seemed to be rocking – to and fro, to and fro – like a cradle hung from a bough in the firmament.

> *Jesus, our brother, strong and good,*
> *Was humbly born in stable rude*
> *And the friendly beasts around him stood,*
> *Jesus, our brother, strong and good.*

The parents and children of the congregation who, except for the high notes, had made a good showing in *Royal David's City* and *The First Nowell*, joined in with a modest buzz – nothing ostentatious, nothing to distract from the angelic performance of the choir, just an enthusiastic drone from a hive of giant bees.

"'I," said the donkey, shaggy and brown,'

cried the choir, dashing off on another lap.

'But he's not – he's grey and quite smooth!' said a voice, obviously struggling, but only too surely failing, to be a whisper. A head nudged my arm and a finger a good deal smaller than mine pointed to the crib.

Not for the first time this afternoon, I spoke out of the corner of my mouth, in the manner of a movie villain.

'*Sh!* Don't point!'

'Why not? I had to show you. See, he's quite—'

I turned my head away, hoping to give the impression of one rudely accosted by a stranger.

The choir, magnanimously taking no notice, continued the tale of the beasts.

'I carried his mother up-hill and down,
I carried her safe to Bethlehem town,
I,' said the donkey, shaggy and brown.
'I,' said the cow, all white and red,
'I gave him my manger for his bed,
I gave him my hay to pillow his head,
I,' said the cow, all white and red.

Just then, for some reason – perhaps he had a liking for cows – the smallest news-boy's candle wobbled. Its flicker, reflected in a series of flashes from the bishop's mitre and the copes of the deans, made those seem to wobble, too.

This caught the attention of the second of my three companions. His keen gaze oscillated between mitre and surplice as though he were a scientist and the clergy under a microscope. He reached up an arm as strong as a wrestler's and dragged my head down to his.

'Why,' he asked, 'are they wearing nightgowns? They look like Wee Willie Winkie.'

The bishop's gold crook trembled in the hand of the bishop's chaplain. I dared not catch his eye. So, mutely, with a hunch of my shoulder, I directed the enquirer's gaze to the crib and kept my own fixed firmly upon it.

There was no doubt about it, the ass *was* grey and very smooth, not a hair out of place – indeed, no hair at all. Every figure in the crib was beautifully tailored, sleek and glossy. Even on the human foreheads nothing had cut a furrow.

The rose-bloom faces of the kings gave no hint of the discipline, the labours, that must surely be the lot of any group of Magi.

The shepherds, with their rugged contours, were nearer to reality, though from their combed beards and tidy sheepskins one could see that they had not been entirely disoriented by the tidings of great joy. And if there were a question in them – 'Why us? Why to such simple men so lordly a favour?' – it was very well dissembled.

The lambs in their arms were as smooth as mushrooms, the flock at their heels unruffled. And amid all that froth of fleece, white and metrical as soap-suds, there was no sign of a black lamb.

What more could one ask, at a children's Christmas Eve service? Yet I found that I did indeed want more, especially for the children's sake — faces trodden by crows'-feet, signs of the ferment, one might almost say chaos, that this unprecedented event brought once and ever brings; something of life, even in carven faces, someone out of breath with running, someone stricken with joy.

And I dearly wanted a black lamb. For, without him, where are the ninety and nine? Flocks, like families, have need of their black sheep — he carries their sorrow for them. He is the other side of their whiteness. Does nobody understand, I wondered, that a crib without a black lamb is an incomplete statement?

My glance fell, perhaps accusingly, on the unfortunate bishop and his cronies.

Now, *there* were faces, if you like – scribbled and veined and netted like the inner side of an elm bark. Life had bitten into them with various strong acids – duty, ardour, anxiety; the business of marshalling their co-shepherds, some, perhaps, obstreperous; the awful responsibility of leading their flock to a Promised Land whose geographical position is known to be hazy; the care of their cathedral that, heavy enough in ordinary times, would have been particularly onerous in recent years when, as each bomb fell on the City of London, Job's comforters everywhere declared that the next one – it was a mathematical inevitability – would certainly fall on St Paul's.

The bishop sighed, and I wondered through what town of the mind this paunchy Wee Willie Winkie was running, as his mouth went up and down like a clapper, forming the words of the carol but obviously not singing. At what windows crying? Tapping at what locks?

> *'I,' said the sheep with curly horn,*
> *'I gave him my wool to keep him warm,*
> *He wore my coat on Christmas morn—'*

sang the choir, in a high soprano bleat. Under the glare of the choir-master, the smallest member straightened his candle.

The bishop's mouth confirmed the news, ritually but in silence. There was a tug at my sleeve.

'Look!' said a husky, communicative voice that sent a shudder along the line or candles. 'He's not singing, he's just opening and shutting his—'

'Hush!' I frowned, feeling as I hoped I looked, like a cobra.

But the deed was done. The bishop had heard.

With a start, he rumbled like an old-fashioned calliope, and hurriedly broke into song.

'"I," said the sheep with curly horn,'

he cawed, favouring us with a pontifical stare very far from sheepish.

The congregation, piously buzzing, achieved the optical feat of keeping one eye on its hymn-book and the other on us in a communal glance of reproach.

'*Our* children,' it seemed to say, 'are quiet and well brought up. They know – thanks, of course, to us – how to behave in public places.'

How true, I thought, hanging my head. But the three flocking round me at the crib were serenely unaware of any reprobation. These children didn't even *know* they were in a public place, they had brought their own world with them. It was, so far, the only one they knew and, as usual, they had dragged me into it, willy-nilly, and left me to take the consequences.

"'I," said the dove in the rafters high,'

cooed the choir, in a sudden pianissimo.

The unexpected lull hushed the children and gave me a little breathing space and time to recollect . . .

For all of them, one near and dear to me, and the others his best friends – let us call them X, Y and Z – this service was a great occasion, almost as important as the day when they had first tasted bananas. The war was over, their lives were

settling for the first time into a normal course, and today they were taking part in the traditional ceremony at St Paul's – bringing their own toys to put under the Christmas Tree for the poor children of London.

In the car, on the way to the City, they had argued sanctimoniously as to which was making the greatest sacrifice.

'I have grown out of Finny,' declared X, lovingly stroking a shabby lion, whose one remaining eye hung by a thread. 'But he's still a valuable present. The poor children will be very grateful.'

'But Finny is old – look at his mane! *I've* brought my best new bus!' Y smirked like a pious angel, but added honestly – 'I really prefer my second-best, although it has no paint.'

'I'm giving my mouse,' said Z loudly. Though small, he had the largest voice, deep and full of reverberations. 'I don't play with him any more, he just sleeps under my pillow. He hasn't got a tail, of course, but he's made of very good rubber.'

To prove the truth of this declaration, he jumped the mouse flightily from one hand to the other.

So, bearing these versions of gold, frankincense and myrrh, we hurried up the steps with the decorous churchgoing crowd, past the statue of Queen Anne, who seemed to be waving her sceptre at us, and into the vast shadowy cave of the cathedral.

Our tip-toe footsteps rang on the marble and echoed up to the vault, so that we seemed to be walking in two places at once, down on the floor and up in the dome.

We peered through the soft transparent light. There stood the crib in its candle-glow. A twinkle came from the Christmas Tree which was railed off from the congregation and flanked by two black-gowned vergers – one tall, withdrawn, austere and solemn; the other short and rubicund, with an innocent saucer-shaped face that smiled at all with equal kindness, like a democratic cherub.

Under the tree lay the heaped-up toys, all of them old and battered – dolls and tops and trains and books that had borne the brunt of love and war. Around them lay tidy piles of clothing – pyjamas, jackets, shirts, shoes – outgrown and neatly mended.

The two vergers scurried from tree to railing, receiving the gifts and depositing them.

Some of the children stood watching as their toys sailed away in the black arms. Others thrust their gifts over the railings and turned abruptly away. Did any of them, I wondered, regret the noble deed? Were there some who felt that virtue might be bought at too high a price?

In front of us, a little girl with a doll was being urged onwards by her father.

'Nonsense, Sylvia!' he was saying. 'It's too late

now to change your mind. Remember the poor children!'

Sylvia burst into tears, gave the doll a quick kiss, and with a gesture that Lady Macbeth would have enjoyed, took it viciously by one leg and hurled it at the tall verger. He caught it nimbly, straightened its garments casually – as though it were nothing but a doll! – and carried it away.

Sylvia, sobbing bitterly, was led off to blow her nose and come to her senses behind the statue of the Duke of Wellington.

Watching this scene, I could not help feeling glad that X, Y and Z had brought toys that, on their own showing, they had outgrown. I turned to them with a confident smile, but it froze on my lips when I saw their faces.

Instead of eager looks and outstretched hands, there were three blank staring statues. Nothing breathed from them, either of kindness or ill-will. They had folded themselves

completely away. And the toys had disappeared.

I could, of course, guess where they were, for X's jacket had a Finny-shaped hump; there was a bulge in Y's jersey that looked very like a bus; and Z's hand was in his pocket – beyond doubt clutching the mouse.

I felt the tall verger's eye boring into my back.

'Er – don't you, after all—?' I began uneasily, and left the question in the air.

They shook their heads.

'Finny wouldn't like it,' said X. 'He doesn't care for strangers.'

This from the boy who had outgrown Finny!

With a look of appeal I turned to Y. His smile was equivocal.

'My bus is too big to go through the railings,' he said, mendaciously.

'Well, what about over the top?'

He was shocked at such an ignorant question.

'Buses don't jump,' he explained severely. 'They go along the ground.'

In desperation I turned to Z as one grasping at a straw. But he quickly looked in the other direction and kept his hand in his pocket.

'There are plenty of toys there already,' he said, ringingly. 'They don't need one more mouse.'

There it was — no more to be said. And had there been more I wouldn't have said it. Nobody was going to have to wipe their eyes behind the statue of the Duke of Wellington on my account. A gift must come from the heart or nowhere.

Nevertheless, I chafed a little. What would the vergers think?

The taller one was staring through me as though I were nothing but stained glass. But the saucer-faced cherub understood. He smiled at my shrug of apology and nodded me off to the children.

They were now zig-zagging down the aisle,

accurately performing the knight's move in chess on the black and white squares of marble, their bodies bulging with the ungiven gifts.

O doves, I thought, with the wisdom of serpents! Faced with a situation too difficult to manage, they had calmly, without shame or regret, marched straight out of it.

I followed them, using the rook's move, to what they described as the 'front stalls', assuring them that the improbable half-naked marble figure of Dr Johnson was not Y's uncle about to take a bath; refraining from correcting X when he informed us that St Paul's cathedral was built entirely by birds. I could, in fact, see the half-truth in it.

Wren, he knew was the architect; Francis Bird had made the statue of Queen Anne; he had heard of the Bird Woman who used to sit on the steps, crying 'Feed the birds! Tuppence a bag!'; and he had been brought up on the fairy tales. It would seem logical to such a one to suppose that linnets and thrushes capable of dropping mill-stones on wicked step-mothers would hardly boggle at building a cathedral.

We rattled into the front pew as the colourful crowd by the altar was coming to the end of a psalm. At once the toys, all danger past, came out of their hiding places. Y, as though to celebrate this event, waved his cap and clapped it on his head.

I signalled to him to remove it. He refused. 'Why should I?' he demanded. 'You're wearing yours!'

I felt, and not for the first time, a certain irritation with the Apostle Paul, and his talent for putting one in an awkward predicament. How could I explain that women should cover their hair and men not? I would only be confronted with another 'why?'

So I pretended not to hear and floated away to my childhood. There I sat, in our family pew, enduring my Sunday furbelows because of my new blue sash. I had edged the big bow round from the back and draped it across my stomach. My mother, listening to the sermon, caught sight of it out of the corner of her eye and twitched it into its proper place. I pulled it round again; and we spent the rest of the service, one hauling the bow to the front, the other jerking it back, till she, losing all patience, hissed – 'It's not *supposed* to be worn like that!'

'Why not?' I said, with an answering hiss. Then I saw the doubt creep into her eyes – did it really matter, one way or the other? – and knew that she was floored.

So *she* pretended not to hear and for self-protection floated off to sit beside *her* mother. And soon, perhaps, she, too, said 'Why?' and her mother floated swiftly away; and then *her* mother, and then and then—

I had almost returned to the Garden of Eden when a stertorous gossiping at my side dragged me back to St Paul's.

'God can do anything. He can fizzle up the world in a frying pan.'

'No, he's not married, the angels do the cooking.'

'What I would like for Christmas is a black dog and a white dog like the ones on the whiskey bottle.'

'*My* mother says *I* can have a pen-knife – but then, *she's* pre-war!'

I was pondering on what, at this period of time, a mother could possibly be like who was *not* pre-war, when the psalm rose grandly to its concluding affirmation.

'Glory be to the Father and to the Son and to the Holy Ghost. As it was in the beginning—'

A skinny arm came round my neck and Z, putting his mouth to my ear in the erroneous belief that he was whispering, crowed piercingly, 'Do you believe in ghosts? I don't!'

Something carried the words round the cathedral. They hooted like owls from wall to pillar and the echoes came flying back from the dome – 'Ghosts! Ghosts! To-whit, To-whoo! I don't, do you?'

Good heavens, we were sitting at the very lip of a microphone!

Luckily, at that moment, the organ rushed to our assistance, drowning the cries in what seemed like a sonorous burst of applause. The choir and clergy, as though a dyke had broken, came surging down among us.

We worked our way along behind them, not pushing anyone but at the same time firmly making sure that nobody pushed *us*. And thus, by courteous stone-walling, we established ourselves in the position we now held, right in front of the crib . . .

My breathing space over, my thoughts came back to the present moment and found that the children were singing and all was well.

'I,' said the dove, in the rafters high,
'I cooed him to sleep with lullaby—'

Finny rocked gently in his master's arms. Z's hand made a cradle for his mouse.

'We cooed him to sleep, my mate and I,
I,' said the dove, in the rafters high.

Then, with magnificent rumpus, the organ sent forth a great volley and every heart seemed audibly to beat a little louder.

The bishop, now on his mettle, was singing as if he meant it, and the choir and congregation were all away together on the last verse, lifting it up so strongly that the roof was almost blown off.

Then every beast by some good spell
In the stable dark was glad to tell
Of the gift he gave Immanuel,
Of the gift he gave Im-man-nu-el.

The faces of the congregation were one big communal gleam. Proud of ourselves as Chanticleers, we mopped an eye here and a nose there, glad that we could all be singing together with the lights on and the storm past.

Fed with good tidings and hungry for tea, the crowd shuffled towards the doors, shoulders rubbing companionably as arms reached out to the vergers' plates and the silver pieces chinked.

Out now in the misty dusk, we stood for a moment on the steps waiting for the bells.

Then they sounded – beating, battering, chiming, changing – a melodious outcry, a musical uproar. For the first time since the war the Christmas peal was ringing! The bells threshed and struck the air – *concord, harmony, unison, peace*! Thongs of music whipped about us, lashed us with joy, smote us with sorrow. *Hear our cry, open your hearts! Ding-dong, ding-dong, this is our song!*

There was no holding the children. They swooped like pigeons down the steps; shouting and singing, they soared away across the street to an alley that led to fields of rubble. When I caught up with them they were dancing to the sound of bells on what had once been a marble floor.

Wherever the bombs fell in London, reinforcements in the shape of sycamore, rose-bay willow, and fern came to fill the gaps. And here was a platoon of green, pushing strongly through the cracks and waving late leaves above the children. There was even an ancient deserted bird's nest.

What had been here – some stately office? A bank? A merchant's hall? And before that, what? I wondered. If it is true the print and form of things remains for ever, as they say, invulnerable and invisible – surely these children were dancing now through long forgotten board-meetings, and shades of accountants, lawyers, clerks. Or, if one went back further, through the flames of the Fire of London, in 1666. Further still, the marble floor would be mud and marshland and all around us brontosaurs; and beyond that we would whirl in lava, turning fierily through the air, nothing but elements.

Contrariwise, would not the City lords to come, in rooms that would rise from this fern and rubble, start up in astonishment at the fancied sight of willow-herb breaking through the carpet? And old cashiers scratch their heads, wondering if they were out of their wits or whether they had really seen three little boys run *through* the cash desk? Are we here? Are we there? Is it now? Is it then? They will not know. And neither do we.

'Hold him for me, please,' said X, breathlessly, as he ran to give me Finny. He was just about to skip back to his friends when a thought struck him.

'Why weren't there any *wild* animals at the crib? Haven't *they* got something to give?'

Under the bells the willow-weed trembled, under the weed the coal forests, under the forests the brontosaurs. The light we stood in was starlight and lamplight, flamelight from the Great Fire and marsh-light from the early ooze before the earth was set. And I heard myself say – 'Yes, they have. And perhaps there is a missing verse.'

'Tell us,' he said, plumping down on a nearby stone and patting the stump of a marble pillar in a gesture of invitation. The other two tumbled upon me, like puppies.

Was it true, what I told them? Did I dream it?

Where it came from I do not know – does anyone, I wonder? – but I seemed to remember every word, just as if I had heard it . . .

. . . It was late at night. Across the way, the inn was quiet. Silence had dropped like a stone into the stable, spreading out ring on ring of stillness, away to the fields and the farthest hills. All was peaceful without and within.

A faint glow came from the centre of the stable, but beyond that all was shadow. The three kings, relaxed and weary after their long journey, dozed among cobwebs in a corner. About them lay a glowing litter, amethyst-and-ruby crowns, velvet cloaks, jewelled stirrups and luminous alabaster boxes that held the kingly gifts.

Nearby, the shepherds, their fleecy cloaks

drawn over their heads, sprawled in one another's laps or leaned against the piled-up hay.

Outside, the angels, poised in the air above the roof-top, were resting from their songs of praise.

The glow in the stable came from the manger, where the Child, a shadow in the midst of his own shine, lay quietly in the straw. Around him stood the friendly beasts, their foreheads drooping upon their chests, their hooves planted sturdily among the scattered sheaves. They were peaceful and still, like furry statues – so still, you would have thought they were far away in the deepest slumber, beyond dreams, aware of nothing. But animals sleep with one ear pricked. They are creatures of earth and it is their nature to listen for the smallest of earth's tremors.

Presently, each of those listening ears gave an imperceptible twitch. The beasts as they dozed had caught the vibration of an almost soundless sound. Even the young lambs sleeping in the crooks of the shepherds' arms heard it; and two of them, a white lamb and a black one, pushed their noses out from under a cloak and sniffed enquiringly.

The sound, too delicate to be heard by human ear, came slowly nearer. A cautious, deliberate padding became every second more audible as it approached the stable. The watchful creatures realised that soft, discreet, determined paws were walking the earth toward them. And presently, as the moon came sliding out of a cloud, they saw, picking his way through the spangled fields, one foot after the other making a faint flowerlike imprint in the frost – a small red fox.

As he came on, pointing his sharp nose along the earth as though following a scent, the farmyard creatures stiffened. They were all aware now, and wary. Their ancient enemy was at hand and

they knew from experience that little good would come of it.

On came the fox, his nostrils trembling eagerly, as he drew near to the stable. Then, as the shine from the manger fell on him, he lifted his head and paused in the doorway, letting out his breath in a long slow sigh. Without glancing to right or left, his yellow far-apart eyes took in the scene and brightened as though he had found what he was looking for.

The young lambs baa-ed nervously, the dove in the rafters gave an anxious chirp.

The fox made no move. For a long time he stood there looking at the crib. Then, without attempting to come farther into the stable, he sat down with a light thud upon his haunches and went on gazing at the manger.

The flanks of the farmyard animals quivered, the straw rustled under their hooves.

But the fox took no notice. He seemed not to know – or, if he knew, not to care – that there was any creature in the place except himself. He swept his tail about him like a great red feather and kept his eyes on the Child.

The throats of the watchers rumbled. Hooves shuffled warningly. Again the straw crackled. But the fox did not move. You would have thought he was all alone in the universe, not a blink, not a flicker.

The animals looked at each other. What was he up to now, they wondered. Then, the ass, with a loud bray, tossed his head.

'Out, fox!' he roared at the newcomer. 'This is no place for you!'

'Be off!' said the cow, angrily mooing.

'Away with you!' the sheep bleated.

'Away, away!' the dove echoed, wildly flapping his wings.

The fox twitched an ear, He curled his white-tipped brush more tightly about his thin black legs. Then slowly, as though he were fetching his attention from a great distance, he turned his head. His narrow eyes blinked as they took in the group of wrathful creatures who watched him from the shadows. He gave his shoulders a little shrug and the red fur rippled along his spine.

'On the contrary,' he said quietly. 'It is the only place for me.'

The ass's tail twitched ominously. His hind legs stamped in the straw.

'Do not try our patience too far, Reynard! We should be loath to use them on such a night but – I warn you! – our hooves are hard.'

The fox, without stirring, looked thoughtfully at the swinging tail and the strong menacing legs.

'Reynard you called me, and that is my name. But if you use it to threaten me, ass, I bid you remember its meaning. It comes from *Raginohardus*, a name that means "strong in counsel".'

The ass gave a loud jeering laugh. 'And what is your counsel, learned sir? To cajole, bamboozle,

dupe, delude? Be off with you, Ragino-hardus! There is no need here for you or your counsel.'

'Who bids me come and go?' asked the fox. 'A lion who speaks with the voice of a mule? Tell me, O mighty lord in a halter, why this should be a place for you—' His glance measured the stable. 'For ass, for cow, for sheep, for dove, and not a place for me?'

'We are here to cherish him,' said the ass, nodding with dignity at the Child.

'And to love him,' murmured the cow gently, with a placid glance at her manger.

The fox appeared to consider this, bending his head sideways as he turned it over in his mind.

'Of love,' he said thoughtfully at length, 'I can say nothing. It is always better not told. But as to cherishing him, why should I not do that as well as you?'

'We are the friends of man,' said the cow. 'You are his enemy.'

'Can friendship be bought?' enquired the fox. 'Does Farmer Two-Legs cosset you for your sake of his bumpkin self? For the drawn cart, the filled churn, the pigeon pie and the shorn fleece, he pays you with an armful of hay and a bit of rope for tether. This might be called a bargain price were it not that, for good measure, he throws in a little sop of sweetness – he calls himself your friend!

'But when was man ever a friend to me? Not

this side of Eden, I assure you. If I am his enemy, he is mine. He puts a price upon my head and I put one on his. When he ties a burning torch to my tail, I run with it through his ripe corn turning the grain to ash. When he waits for me with a gun in the covert, I double back to the farmhouse kitchen and steal his new-smoked hams. No fox was ever a friend to man. And yet—' a shadow darkened the yellow eyes. 'One fox, when the time comes, will be man's friend. I shall be a friend to one man only, though he is not yet grown.'

'Impossible!' declared the sheep. 'You cannot do anything but cheat. Remember how you tricked the crow! And Chanticleer, the great cock! And the poor goat in the well!'

At that the fox smiled. 'Foolish creatures, I remember them well. They did not trouble to think for themselves. They deserved what they got.'

'Chicken thief! Robber of nests! You and the

cuckoo are a pair!' the dove complained, shaking its wings.

'Chickens are made to be stolen,' said the fox. 'There are millions of chickens in the world, none of them of any more use than to have its bones picked. And – speaking comparatively, of course – the world has very few foxes. As for the cuckoo, we do indeed make a good pair – when I have eaten one for my supper!'

'You live by cunning!' the ass accused him.

'What moralists you all are! What else should I live by? Tell me that! How else should I distinguish, on a spring evening, the broken bough and the crossed sticks that say where the trap is set? What else will tell me, as I hunt along the furrow in summer, that the dead hare stretched there has a heart packed with poison? What warns me in autumn to hide my cubs deep underground and cheat the early huntsman? What takes me off down-wind in winter away from the ravening hounds? My cunning – only my cunning.'

46

'You have never learned to serve,' said the cow.

'I serve myself,' said the fox, serenely. 'And my vixen when she calls to me with her double bark across the hills. And my cubs, when I feed them on wren and partridge, until they can creep to the hen-roosts themselves.'

'That is thieving. That is not serving man,' the cow argued.

'You speak like a slave,' said the fox, mildly. 'Man, man, always man! Is there no other living thing? What of the forests no man has seen – do they not still go on growing? Will the fire at the core of the earth go out because man cannot warm his hand at it? I serve, as man himself serves. I breathe in, I breathe out. What I take in from air, the earth takes in from me. But what it is I serve, I do not know. I am a fox, not a philosopher. I have four feet, not two.'

'The same old wily words, Reynard,' taunted the ass. 'But they will not help you here. In this

place, there is no room for those who have nothing to offer and nothing to share. You take, you do not give. You think of nothing but yourself, always yourself alone.'

'Forcible reasoning, Comrade Hee-Haw!' mocked the fox. 'And indeed I do not dispute it. Always myself alone,' he repeated, with a note of joy in his voice. 'Myself alone dancing at the edge of the clearing, not for anyone's pleasure but my own. No one bids me go here, go there. The king's candle and the beggar's both shine gold but neither beckons me under a roof. I live in danger, as the halcyon lives that builds her nest on the wave; alone with myself at all times, when the wind rises and the rain comes down. Yes, and under the snow! To be alone is my nature. It is also my nature – you have said it – to share nothing. What is mine, I keep. When I pick a bone, I pick it dry, as brittle as a dead elm-twig. I have or have not, according to fate and season – and either way it is whole. Half a thing is no use to me.'

His gaze, without shame or reproach, moved tranquilly from one animal to another. 'Have you anything else against me?'

'You have a strong, red, foxy smell,' said the dove, sniffing the air.

'I admit it,' replied the fox. 'I am compost, not flower.'

'You take our lambs,' the sheep accused him.

A dreamy reminiscent look came into the fox's eyes and he ran his tongue over his lips as though he were thinking of something delicious.

'I have to eat to live,' he said, smiling. 'It is true, however, that I am no fit company for anything that bleats.'

'You cannot be tamed,' said the cow, reproachfully.

'If you mean,' the fox answered, 'that I do not willingly wear a collar, you are stating a simple fact. Nor would I agree, in my right mind, to living in a barn. What would it profit me to run with the flock, shoulder to shoulder with woolly

brother, when all it leads to is the basting dish? When they put me in a cage I waste away, running from corner to corner. I bite the hand that feeds me when that hand puts a chain on my neck. No one, indeed, can tame a fox. And yet,' the yellow eyes darkened, 'the time is coming when a fox shall be tamed.'

The animals stared suspiciously. What roguery was he planning now?

'And when will that be?' they all jeered.

The fox was silent for a moment. Then he turned his head towards the manger and gave a little nod.

'When I have given him my gift,' he said.

'Oho, Reynard,' the ass snorted. 'Have you suddenly learnt to share? Fool us no more with your double tongue. What gift could you give to him?'

'It was not sudden,' the fox said, coolly. 'I was a long time coming to it and it was not easy.'

'Is it your coat?' the sheep demanded. 'If

so it is far too coarse and prickly. Besides, I have already given him my wool to keep him warm.'

'It is not my coat,' the fox assured her.

'Your lair,' asked the cow, for him to sleep in? I fear a fox-hole would smell too strong. Apart from that, as you will have observed, his bed is in my manger.'

'It is not my lair,' replied the fox.

'You are not assuming, Reynard, surely,' scoffed the ass, 'that you could carry him about! That is *my* job. I have already brought his mother a long way – out of Egypt, uphill and down – and my back is broad enough for any burden he is likely to put upon it.'

The fox regarded him quizzically.

'My spine is strong and flexible. But no such thing was in my mind.'

The dove strutted and preened her wings.

'You are not proposing to sing to him, you with your grating voice? If so, fox, you must think again. I have already sung him my lullaby and I shall do it again.'

'I am no songster,' said the fox, smiling. But the smile faded as he looked from one animal to another.

'So bounteous — and yet so jealous!' he said, shaking his head. 'Do not be disturbed, my friends. What I have for him is mine alone. It will not lessen the value of your gifts.'

'Let us judge of that for ourselves,' brayed the ass. 'Just tell us what it is.'

The fox looked at them reflectively for a moment. Then he gave a little shrug.

'My cunning,' he said.

The animals stared, amazed and outraged. The fox calmly returned their stare.

'Good!' said a voice from the manger.

Their heads went up as one head. And as though there were but a single mind between them, they turned to the crib and saw that the Child had raised his hand. He was looking at them

with clear bright eyes and smiling with great kindness.

'That is a good gift,' he said gravely, glancing towards the fox.

The ass snorted. He was perplexed. 'Why is it good?' he demanded, obstinately. 'You are young and true and innocent. What need have you of cunning?'

'It is good,' said the Child, 'because it is not half a thing. It is whole. Who else among you has given me as much? The kings—' he smiled across at the dozing Magi. 'The kings have given me rare gifts – pure metal, sweet resin, fragrant oil – but, being wise men, they are also rich men. And wisdom is inexhaustible. They can never lose what they give away.

'The shepherds have brought me their young lambs, as suitable to my state. But this does not deplete their flocks. When spring comes the ewes will suckle many more. There are always lambs abounding.

'The cow, indeed, has given me her manger. But soon I shall be too big for it and the farmer will fill it again with corn.

'As for the ass – beyond question, he carried my mother a long way and the time will come – I warn him now! – when he must carry me, too, among the palms and shouting. But for all that, his back is not broken. It will still bear other burdens.

'When the dove sang me her lullaby, it was not the end of her singing. There will be other children to coo to sleep and brood after brood of nestlings.'

His eyes turned toward the sheep.

'You gave me your coat to keep me warm. But you will grow another as the seasons pass. That is the way of sheep. All of you – and I thank you – have given me gifts that still remain your own. That is as it should be for in this way we can share them together. But the fox—'

The Child paused, and the light about him glowed more brightly.

'The fox has given me all he had. Without his cunning, how will he find food or escape the snare? How will he live now, alone in the woods? His cunning is his strength, his cunning is his life. It is the only thing he has and he has given it away.'

'But what will you do with such a gift?' cried the ass, in bewilderment. 'I am puzzled at these riddles. What is this cunning? There is something here I do not understand.'

'Nor I!' echoed the cow, the sheep and the dove, doubtfully shaking their heads.

'It is not necessary to understand,' said the Child, gently. 'It is only necessary to let it be. Love and let be.'

Then he turned his head toward the door and beckoned to the fox.

'Come!' he commanded.

The fox nodded obediently. And, delicately lifting each paw and putting it down without a sound, he stepped up to the manger.

The Child put out his hand and laid it on the red head in the broad space between the ears.

'I come from beyond the world,' he said. 'If I must live in a strange land, I shall need some one to help me.'

The fox made a curious sound in his throat, something between a growl and a groan.

'What would you have me do?' he cried. 'Roll you under the thorn with my paw, as I do my half-grown cubs? Follow the cry of the night-owl, wrest her prey from her sharp claws and feed you with a fine fat squirrel? Hide you in my fox's hole and when they hunt you – as hunt they will! – lead you by the secret paths that no one knows but I?'

'Stay with me,' the Child pleaded. 'They give me Christmas welcome now. But some day, when the leaves are green, it will be a different story. Raginohardus, be my friend. Let it be you and I together!'

The fox, his eyes glistening, let his head rest for a moment only beneath the hand of the Child. Then he bent it sideways and away.

'You know I cannot do that,' he said. 'That would make two of us. You come, indeed, from beyond the world. Therefore, you know well that what you have to do can only be done by one. Do not tempt me. I am your friend, and for that reason I must refuse to be your friend, no matter what it costs me. Let me go. What a friend could do, I have done already. I have given you my cunning – and much good may it do you! It is you who are the fox now, alone against the world.'

The Child trembled. He looked away quickly as though unwilling to understand the fox's words. For a time he seemed to be lost in his own thoughts. But presently he nodded to himself – slowly, sadly, one, two, three – as though in his heart he had accepted a very difficult thing.

'You are right,' he whispered. 'That is how it must be – alone when the wind rises and the rain comes down.'

'And under the snow,' the fox added. 'I will go and live in the hedgerows.'

As he spoke, he moved his body away – very slowly, inch by inch – so that the Child's hand slid down the length of his red back and along the brush to the last hair. It seemed as though neither could bear to part from the other.

Then, with a sigh, the fox flung up his head abruptly and thrusting himself away from the manger, he padded with dainty purposeful steps

over the straw to the farmyard animals. With grave deliberation, he chose a place between the cow and the ass and lay down, curling his brush about him, and sliding his pointed mask along his paws.

The young black lamb, who had watched the scene in silence, crept out from under the shepherd's cloak, staggered clumsily across the stable and settled itself beside the fox, leaning its dark muzzle on the sleek red flank.

But the fox took no notice. His yellow eyes were fixed unblinkingly upon the Child and the Child's eyes shone unblinkingly back at him. With a look that seemed to unwind time the two gazed at each other. What they said in that look no one can tell. They might have lived a lifetime in it – thirty-three years of life, maybe – stretching away from this winter night to a far-off day in spring.

The other animals, without knowing why, felt their anger melt away. 'We are too simple to understand,' they thought to themselves. 'We can only love and let be.'

So, flooded with a humble joy, they pondered on the night's events, and drew nearer to the fox as they pondered. And after a while, for they were not used to thinking things out, they nodded drowsily, and then awoke to ponder again, and nodded again and slept.

And so the night turned. The kings, in a scatter of gold and jewels, dozed in their shadowy corner. The shepherds snored softly into their beards.

Outside in the sky, the bright star above the stable spun on its axis with a steady hum. Angels and archangels, in a trance, swung like pendulums in the air, resting their cheeks on their harps.

The town slept, ringing the stable round. And all that ringed the town around lay in a tranquil slumber.

But the Child and the fox were both awake, gazing at each other. Silently, sleeplessly, without stirring, as though they two were alone on the

earth, they looked at each other and kept their watch all through the moving night.

This is the way the wheel turns, coming at last to full circle, with wild as well as tame at the crib; lion and turtle-dove together and barnyard beasts lying down with the fox. For wild and tame are but two halves and here, where all begins and ends, everything must be whole.

And always, among the sleepers, there must be somebody waking – somewhere, someone, waking and watchful. Or what would happen to the world ... ?

'Would it stop spinning, do you think?' an attentive voice enquired.

I swam up swiftly through time and space and

broke the surface at the field of rubble. There I was, still seated on the broken marble with the three listeners sprawled beside me. Around us waved the willow-herb — was there a red fox flitting through it? — and up in the air with relentless clamour, the bells of St Paul's were still ringing.

'Well, would it?'

But who could answer such a question — certainly not I! Besides, it was far too cold for questions. I pulled them all from their stone perches and we ran beneath the changing chimes, like dancers under maypole ribbons, and found the car and drove away with the ringing echoes in our ears.

The City was full of cheerful people, all glad to be walking on the pavements, instead of hiding under them. And weaving through the winding streets the children savoured the experience of driving home, for the first time, by lamplight. Our mood was calm and companionable, with X and Y carrying on a friendly altercation and Z sitting silent beside me, like a placid brooding bird.

'What would a tiger give?' asked Y. And then withdrew the question. The general feeling seemed to be that the tiger was too fierce for the stable and the best place for him the jungle.

The lion, however, was nobler, or at least amenable to reason. X was of the opinion that the lion would give his strength, and Y capped this with the elephant who, on hearing of the great event, hurried to offer the Child his trunk.

And so it went on, a long procession of birds and beasts drifting towards us and away, each with its gift for the Child. The giraffe, because of his long neck, plucked down the juiciest fruit from the tree-tops; the whale, thanks to the grating in his throat, was able to catch a shoal of fish and present them, fully fried; the magpie, with its magpie chatter, brought him the daily news; and the pig relinquished one of his ears to make a new silk purse – I having once remarked, in the teeth of the proverb, that, properly worked on, a sow's ear will make a purse worthy of any silkworm. Sparrows came with a gift of crumbs; the lordly peacock spread out his tail and gave the Child a lucky peacock feather.

Their philanthropy was as boundless as their invention. Hearing them talk, an outsider would have had to declare that here were a couple of archangels. Such a one would never guess that the battered lion and the shiny bus, now royally riding back to Chelsea instead of sitting in St Paul's, were mute but vital evidence of their paragon owners' lapse in virtue.

Nevertheless, the charity that had not begun at

home was expansive and large-hearted when it came to imagining the gifts the beasts would give. It was not vicarious generosity. In the world of childhood there is no sharp cleavage between four legs and two. And in designing a course of conduct for the animals X and Y were, in their own way, adjusting the balance, giving what humanly *could* be given, everything but the last, lone treasure – not Finny, not the bus.

It is true, when you come to think of it, that there are, indeed, very few foxes!

The naming of beasts and gifts continued. The boys were so absorbed in their good deeds that even the enormous tree, blazing with stars in Trafalgar Square, came as an anti-climax. On hearing it had been sent by Norway, they murmured vaguely 'How kind of him!' and went on with their dream.

They were shaken out of it, however, by the sight of *several* Father Christmases walking among the crowds around the tree. This, to them,

was a clear case of misrepresentation and a matter for indignation. Everyone knew there was only one! There were, they understood, certain children who didn't believe even that, but insisted that Father Christmas was really only your mother. These were held to be misinformed, and X scoffed loudly at such an idea.

'*My* mother *never* comes down the chimney! It would make her far too dirty.' The undeniable truth of this met with general approval.

'Besides' added Y, with perfect logic. 'Father Christmas is not a lady!' He brooded for a moment. 'I wonder what present he'll bring tomorrow – I mean, to the boy in the stable.'

Pondering on the question, I thought – as I had so often thought before – that though the frontiers of childhood are wide and flexible, its laws are strict and fixed. All time, all space is one there, and nothing is incongruous – not even the idea that the hero whom the children knew at this moment to be whipping up his reindeers should have a present in his sack for the Child of long ago. In that world, Father Christmas is indistinguishable from the three kings, for everything that was, is always. Two thousand years ago is now, fact and fable are both true and nothing separates them.

What, indeed! Y had set us all wondering and Z, who had taken no part in the game, woke up from his cogitations and croakily broke the silence.

'I liked that lost verse,' he said shyly, in his hoarse sweet, raven voice as he ran his rubber mouse round the car-wheel.

It was at that moment we saw the swan.

She was flying along the Mall towards us, her wings swinging up and down in a large majestic movement. She passed us, white in the grey light, sweeping just above our heads with a hollow rushing sound.

A swan, in London, a wild swan – flying so low that she almost touched us! Such an event was all we needed to complete the day's adventure.

But why had she chosen this evening, we wondered. What was she doing, all alone, and where was she coming from?

X and Y thought it probable that she had been on a visit to Buckingham Palace for tea with the king and queen.

But Z knew better. He had no doubts.

'She's not coming from anywhere. She's going *there*!' he said.

No one said 'where?' We all knew. Z had completed the story for us. She was going to join the fox.

'But how will she know the right way?' Y, with

his scientific bent, was all a thirst for detail. 'Does anyone know where the stable is?'

'It's not on any map,' said X, flinging me a large blue look, full of the experience of his short, abundant life. 'It's at the end of the world.'

Y, accepted this calmly. It was just a factual statement. 'And what will she give him, do you think?'

I reminded them of the old legend how before she dies the swan sings once – her first song and her last.

'So, you see, she will give him her swan-song.'

X and Y agreed to this. And the mouse ran round and round the wheel, delighted at the prospect.

The swan was climbing higher now, breasting the Admiralty Arch and bearing towards the east. She would fly, I thought, along the river, with the City spreading out before her and St Paul's bells beating under her wings. Soon she would be beyond the coast, with the earth revolving slowly

below her – oceans, capes and continents, lakes and peaks and forests.

But the children thought otherwise. To say simply 'peak' or 'ocean' was not sufficiently exact. The swan would want them named.

She would go by the hymn-book lands, they insisted, and they set her – all from memory – upon her proper course. It led above the bright blue sky to Greenland's icy mountains and on to gold Jerusalem, drenched with its milk and honey. From there it would take her past all things bright and beautiful, to Canaan's pleasant land. On, still onwards, it would lead, over living fountains, rocks of ages and pastures where the young lambs are safe from all-alarms. And at last, when day was over and the night drawing nigh, she would come to the green hill far away, to the stable that lies at the world's end, beyond the hills of glory, beyond the jasper sea.

It was, indeed, a boundless journey, with its paths meeting again and again as the paths of wild creatures in the woods cross and re-cross each other.

A long way and yet no distance. The end of the world is hard to find, but it may be as near as it is far, east of the sun and west of the moon or just around the corner.

By the time we were home and had lit the fire, the swan would be with the fox ...

Chelsea, London, May, 1962

Aunt Sass
Christmas Stories

P. L. Travers

*With a foreword by Victoria Coren Mitchell
and illustrations by Gillian Tyler*

In the 1940s P. L. Travers wrote three stories which she gave as Christmas gifts to her friends. Virago has published them for the first time.

Friends come in many guises. In these autobiographical stories the narrator looks back over her childhood and remembers three characters whose influence has lasted a lifetime: an irascible but lovable great aunt, a Chinese cook and a foul-mouthed ex-jockey. Each enters her life just when she needs them most. And each, however unlikely, becomes a friend and champion of the young girl – especially Aunt Sass, the inspiration for Mary Poppins.

Charming, tender and moving these stories contain all the hallmarks you'd expect from this spellbinding writer.